# Yankee Doodle

**Repeat this melody for each verse in the song.**

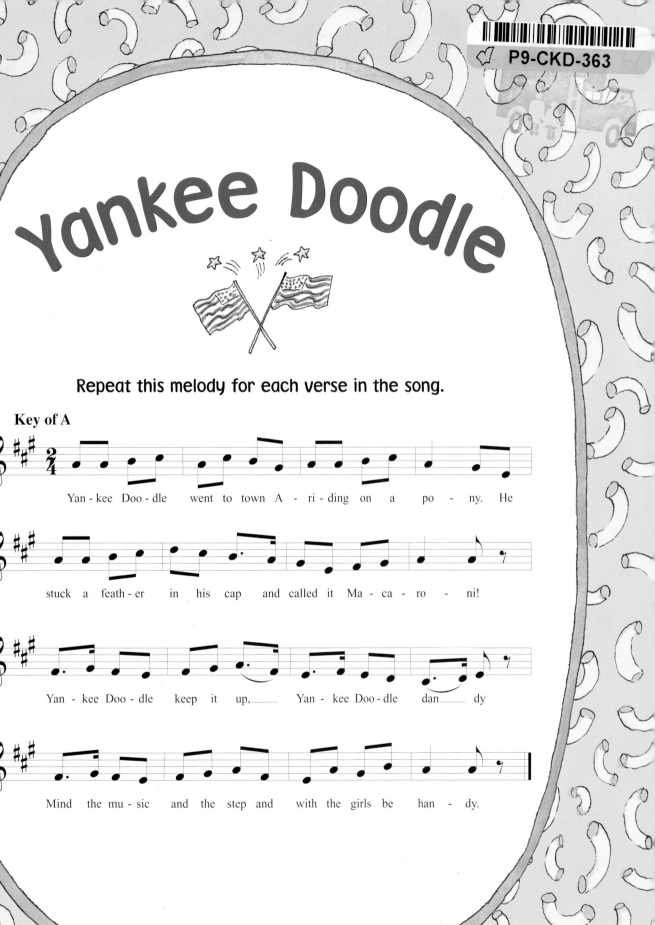

Key of A

Yan - kee Doo - dle went to town A - ri - ding on a po - ny. He

stuck a feath - er in his cap and called it Ma - ca - ro - ni!

Yan - kee Doo - dle keep it up,____ Yan - kee Doo - dle dan___ dy

Mind the mu - sic and the step and with the girls be han - dy.

—N.B.W.

For Wendy and Dennis

To Julia, John, George, and Laura Gallagher

—M.A.H.

Text copyright © 2004 by Mary Ann Hoberman
Illustrations copyright © 2004 by Nadine Bernard Westcott
Sing-Along Stories Series Editor, Mary Ann Hoberman
More fun with Yankee Doodle! Activity Page © 2004 by
Little, Brown and Company (Inc.)

First Edition

The Sing-Along Stories logo design is a trademark of Little, Brown and Company (Inc.).

Library of Congress Cataloging-in-Publication Data

Hoberman, Mary Ann.
   Yankee Doodle /[adapted by] Mary Ann Hoberman ; [illustrations by] Nadine Bernard Westcott. — 1st ed.
      p. cm.
   "Megan Tingley books."
   Summary: Expands on the familiar song to include a girl, a poodle, a toad, and a rooster who, along with
Yankee Doodle, open a restaurant called Yankee Doodle's Noodles.
Includes music.
   ISBN 0-316-145513
   1. Children's songs — Texts. [1. Songs.] I. Westcott, Nadine Bernard, ill. II. Title.
PZ8.3.H66 Yan 2004
782.42'083 — dc21                                                                                       2003040024

10 9 8 7 6 5 4 3 2 1

Book design by Alison Impey

SC

Manufactured in China

The illustrations for this book were done in watercolor and ink.
The text was set in Claude Sans, and the display type is Fontoon ITC.

# Yankee Doodle

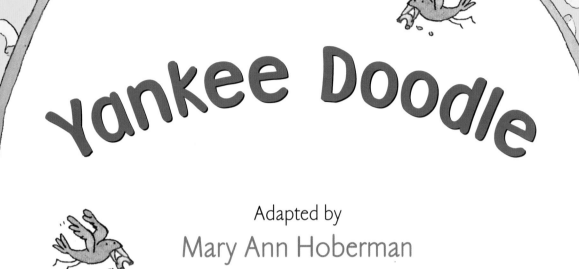

Adapted by
## Mary Ann Hoberman

Illustrated by
## Nadine Bernard Westcott

Sing-Along Stories Series Editor, Mary Ann Hoberman

Megan Tingley Books
## LITTLE, BROWN AND COMPANY
New York ❦ An AOL Time Warner Company

Yankee Doodle went to town
A-riding on a pony.
He stuck a feather in his cap
And called it Macaroni!

Yankee Doodle keep it up,
Yankee Doodle dandy,
Mind the music and the step
And with the girls be handy!

Yankee Doodle met a girl
A-walking with a poodle.
Good-day, said he, please ride with me.
My name is Yankee Doodle.

The girl she laughed to hear his name
And jumped up on his saddle.
The poodle followed close behind
And off they did skedaddle.

Then on the road they met a toad.
The toad hopped on the feather.
What fun, they cried, come join our ride!
And off they rode together.

A fine old rooster came along
A-singing cock-a-doodle.

He flapped his wings and flew straight up
And landed on the poodle.

The pony pranced.  The poodle danced.
The girl gave out some candy.
Oh, what a merry band are we!
Cried Yankee Doodle Dandy.

I still am hungry, said the toad.
I'm hungry, said the pony.
I'm hungry, too, the rooster said.
Let's have some macaroni.

Then someone got a good idea
(Perhaps it was the poodle's)
To open up a restaurant
Called Yankee Doodle's Noodles.

Toad and pony were the cooks.
The waiter was the poodle.

The girl and rooster made dessert,

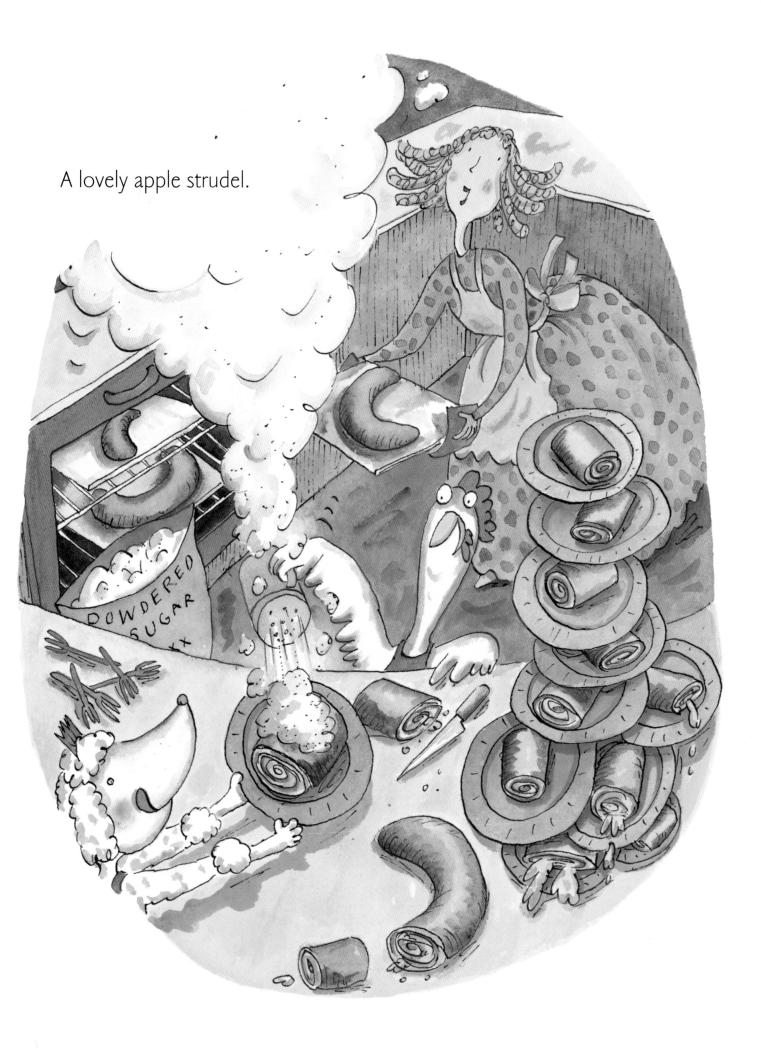

A lovely apple strudel.

They also sold cold lemonade,
Salami and baloney,

But best of all, their customers
Liked cheese and macaroni.

AH-CHOOo!

MENU
cold lemonade
salami
baloney
apple strudel
cheese and
macaroni

Oh, how they ate! They cleaned each plate!
They gulped and gobbled oodles!
They'd never munched so fine a lunch,
Especially the noodles.

And on the fourth day of July,
Along with Yankee Doodle,
The friends all led a big parade,
The whole kit and caboodle.

They marched along and sang this song
With Yankee and his pony,
And each one wore a feathered cap
And called it Macaroni!

Yankee Doodle keep it up,
Yankee Doodle dandy,
Mind the music and the step
And with the girls be handy!

# More fun with *Yankee Doodle*!

① Count and name the characters that ride on Yankee Doodle's pony. Which is the largest? Which is the smallest? Draw a picture of the pony and add three more characters. How many characters are on the pony in your picture?

② Macaroni and Cheese is the favorite food at Yankee Doodle's Noodles. Suppose Yankee Doodle sells a bowl of macaroni and cheese for 25 cents. How much money does he make if he sells 6 bowls at lunch?

③ Yankee Doodle and his friends march in a parade at the end of the song. Make a feathered cap like the one Yankee Doodle and his friends wear. Plan a parade with classmates, friends, or family and march to the rhythm of the song as it is sung.

④ Name all the words in the song that rhyme with "doodle." What other rhyming pairs of words are in the song (for example, "dandy" and "handy")? Think of other words to rhyme with each rhyming pair.

⑤ Yankee Doodle's parade takes place on the Fourth of July. Talk about why the Fourth of July is special to our country. Most parades have a marching band to supply the music. Name the instruments that are usually in a marching band. Suggest other songs for the band to play in the parade.

Activities prepared by Pat Scales, Director of Library Services, The South Carolina Governor's School for the Arts and Humanities, Greenville, SC.